ESTHER A.D.

Lydia Eberhardt

ESTHER
A.D.

Lydia Eberhardt

TATE PUBLISHING
AND ENTERPRISES, LLC

Esther A.D.

Published by Tate Publishing & Enterprises, LLC
127 E. Trade Center Terrace | Mustang, Oklahoma 73064 USA
1.888.361.9473 | www.tatepublishing.com

Tate Publishing is committed to excellence in the publishing industry. The company reflects the philosophy established by the founders, based on Psalm 68:11,
"The Lord gave the word and great was the company of those who published it."

Cover & Interior design by Sarah Kirchen

Published in the United States of America

ISBN: 978-1-61346-465-6
1. Fiction / Christian / Historical
2. Fiction / Christian / Futuristic
11.08.18

For Mrs. Falck, my kindergarten teacher,
who gave me the keys
to unlock the world of reading
and instilled in me a love for books.

And for my students,
as I endeavor to do the same.

INTRODUCTION

I have always loved the story of Esther. I've read every version of the story I could find. One evening as I was trying to fall asleep after having finished rereading one of my favorite versions, I was struck with the realization that Esther's story is always set in ancient times. I wondered if it would work in a more modern setting. Soon the story began to form in my mind, and I realized, *Oh, this is pretty good!* I grabbed a notebook and began to frantically write down what would later become chapter six. For several nights following, I lost sleep over this book, not because I couldn't figure out what to write, but because that was when the story took shape.

When I was about halfway through, I asked my friend Bonnie to read it and see what she thought. She loved it and kept encouraging me to write more because she wanted to know what would happen next. I have to say thank you to her, for if it wasn't for her encouragement, this story probably would not have gotten completed, since school started up and I was very busy with a new year of teaching.

But finish it I did, and here is the result.

Enjoy!

ONE

Matthew jumped out of his car and ran down what had only an hour ago been the street where his uncle Abraham lived with his wife and eight-year-old daughter. Now it was a pile of half-burning rubble caused by the bombs of Perea's enemies. The Great Global Wars had reorganized the countries of the world, and even though the wars had ended over one hundred years ago, there were still these attacks as the new countries tried to establish their position in the new world order. *Please have spared them, LORD,* Matthew prayed as he got closer to his uncle's house. The neighbor's house was engulfed in flames, and as he stopped in front of his uncle's house, he saw that a missile had torn through the roof of the house, exploding when it hit the neighbor's. The force of the explosion had collapsed the roof and knocked down several walls, but what was left of the house was not burning, so Matthew's hope began to rise. *It's not completely destroyed. They might have survived.*

"Hello? Can anyone hear me?" he called. He carefully stepped over what had once been a wall, a chair, and a bookshelf. He heard a loud crunch as he stepped on some glass. Matthew looked down and then bent to pick up the picture frame on which he had stepped. The glass was broken, but the picture of his uncle's family still smiled through the broken glass. He removed the picture and dropped the broken frame back into the rubble. "Hello? Is there anyone here?" he called again, tucking the picture into his pocket.

Just then he heard the sound of crying. Matthew jumped over a fallen tree, pushed aside some broken pieces that had been part of the roof, and cried out in joy. For there, in a small cave that had been formed in the collapse, lay his cousin, Hannah, scared and crying, but uninjured.

"Thank you, Lord!" Matthew said. He pulled his young cousin out of the rubble and into his arms.

TWO

FIFTEEN YEARS LATER

"Dignitaries from across the provinces continue to arrive as preparations for Perea's victory celebration continue here in Susa and around the country." Hannah sat forward on the couch to get a better look at the television screen. She watched with wide eyes as the arriving palace guests smiled and waved to the mass of people crowded at the palace gates trying to catch a glimpse of those invited. King Xavier had invited politicians, movie stars, and other celebrities to join him and Queen Valerie at the palace for the celebration.

The anchorwoman continued with her report. "As we all remember, after the defeat and murder of his father, King Xavier vowed revenge on Perea's enemies. Months of negotiating have now been completed after years of skirmishes, followed by three years of declared war. The surrender and peace agreement was officially signed this morning. The weeklong country-wide celebration will officially begin in two days, although some have begun the celebrations early."

The front door banged shut, drawing her attention away from the television. "Hannah, I'm home," called Matthew.

Hannah jumped off the couch and headed down the hallway toward the entryway. "Please, Matthew, you *have* to let me go to the celebration. Everyone in the whole world is going to be there except for me!"

Matthew smiled and kissed her on the forehead. "The whole world, eh? I highly doubt those we defeated will be celebrating our victory. You know that it wouldn't be safe for you to go by yourself. I must be at the palace during the celebration, and I can't take you with me."

"I know, your job at the palace must go on, even during the celebration. But it's just not fair." Hannah pouted, crossing her arms in front of her.

"You're right. It's not fair. Now stop pouting. Can't you see I've brought a guest?" Matthew gestured back toward the doorway where a young man stood.

"Joshua, you're back!" Hannah called out and jumped over to where he stood and gave him a hug. She stepped back and looked him up and down. "I do believe you've grown! Are you sure you're Joshua?" she said teasingly.

Joshua smiled and struck a pose as she looked him over. He had indeed grown. When he had left to join Perea's army, they had been the same height, but now he was several inches taller than she. The training and war had given him a lean, muscular build. His raven hair, which he had always worn slightly long and messy, was now kept neat and short. He then wrinkled his nose and said, "What? Do you not recognize your childhood friend?"

Hannah made a fist and lightly punched him on the arm. "Of course I recognize you, silly. It's just that I've missed my childhood friend since he's been off fighting for our country." She gave him another hug. "I'm so glad you're back safe. We have so much catching up to do."

Suddenly she turned and looked at Matthew. "I have a wonderful idea! I can go to the celebration with Joshua. He'll make sure I don't get into trouble and that I make it home safe. Please? I don't have to go every day, just one day, and there will be fireworks on the last day. There haven't been fireworks in so long." Hannah turned back to Joshua. "Say you'll go with me, please, Josh?" She looked up at him, her green eyes pleading.

Joshua looked up at Matthew. "The whole army has been given leave to attend the celebration. I'll take her with me if you say it's okay." Hannah turned back to Matthew with a hopeful look spread across her face.

Matthew looked back and forth between her and Joshua, weighing the decision in his mind. "Very well," he said finally, "but you must promise me that you'll listen to Joshua and not try and wheedle him into doing whatever you want. You aren't little children anymore."

Hannah's face broke into a giant smile, and she ran and gave Matthew a hug. "Thank you! I promise I will be on my best behavior the whole time!" she said with joy, giving her dear cousin a kiss on the cheek.

Matthew chuckled softly, gently shooing Hannah toward the kitchen. "Now, that's enough of that. Let's get dinner on the table for our guest, and then you two can have some time to catch up."

THREE

The doorbell rang, and Hannah quickly jumped up from the chair she had only seconds before sat down in to answer it. "He's here!" she exclaimed. Matthew rose from his chair and followed her down the hallway to the front door.

"Corporal Joshua David here, reporting for duty, sir!" Joshua said, giving Matthew a salute as he came into the entryway.

"Come on, Joshua. Let's go!" said Hannah, pulling on his other arm.

Matthew returned Joshua's salute and then said, "Well, you better get going before my impatient cousin pulls your arm from its socket."

"Don't worry, Matthew. I'll look after her," Joshua called back to him as he was pulled down the steps and out to his waiting car.

"Have fun!" Matthew waved good-bye. Then he locked the door and turned to go to his own car for his drive to the palace.

A loud pounding on the chamber door awoke Queen Valerie from her sleep. She focused her sleepy eyes on the clock. *Who on earth has the nerve to be pounding on the queen's door at two thirty in the morning?* she thought. She flipped back her blanket, sat up, and rubbed her eyes. She had left the celebration at midnight, and two hours of sleep had not been nearly enough. "Somebody better be dead or dying," Valerie growled as she stumbled to the door. She paused for a moment to run a hand through her hair to remove any tangles that had formed as she slept. Opening the door, she placed a polite smile on her face. "Yes, what is it?" she said to the nervous servant standing before her.

"Your majesty, King Xavier requests your presence at the celebration."

Valerie raised her eyebrows in annoyance. After six days of celebration, she was tired, and with only a couple of hours of sleep, she was in no mood to participate in the complicated dance of politics. "Please give the king my regards, but I won't be returning to the festivities."

Valerie shut the door to her room and rested her head against the door for a moment before walking toward her bed. "Unbelievable," she muttered as she flopped backward onto her bed.

Five minutes later there was a timid knock on her door. Valerie's eyes snapped open. "You've got to be kidding me!" she exclaimed. She stalked back to the door and opened it without a word and fixed her gaze on the servant who stood there, trembling.

"The ki—." The servant's voice caught as he began to speak, so he swallowed and tried again. "The king demands that you return to the banquet. Immediately, Your Majesty," the servant ended quietly, staring at the toes of his shoes.

Valerie stared silently at the servant until he looked up at her. "Will you come?" he asked.

Without a word, Valerie shut the door.

“She has what?” King Xavier roared, catching the attention of all those celebrating nearby.

The trembling servant who had brought the news quietly repeated himself. “She has refused to come, sire, and won’t even open the door anymore.”

The king’s gaze raked across the revelers nearby, all of whom were trying to appear as if they were not listening while in reality they were hanging on every word. He saw Hayden, one of the junior councilmen, standing nearby. “Hayden!” he called.

Hayden moved quickly to the king’s side and bowed, “Yes, sire?” he asked.

“Summon the council, and have them meet me in the conference room. Now!” Hayden bowed again as the king turned and left the room.

It had been three hours since Queen Valerie had refused the king’s demand. The celebration at the palace had ended shortly after the abrupt exit of the king. Those in attendance had quickly and rather quietly left or returned to their rooms in the palace, some to sleep, but many to talk with their friends and neighbors about what had happened.

The council had never assembled so quickly before. King Xavier sat brooding in his chair at the head of the table. His council silently sat in their places around the table, watching him, waiting for him to speak. Hayden stood silently in a shadowy corner, observing them all with shrewd and calculating eyes.

Finally the king spoke. "What should I do about *her?*" he said, unable to bring himself to even say Valerie's name.

The minister of agriculture spoke first. "Perhaps she was just very tired. It has after all been a very long week of celebrations. She probably just needs some rest, and then I'm sure she'll want to apologize."

"That may be," interrupted the minister of communications, "but the damage has already been done. You know how fast news travels these days. The story of the queen's refusal has probably spread throughout the entire country by now!"

Silence fell over the room when he finished speaking. Hayden stepped forward so he could be seen by all and began to speak. "And you know how the women of the country look to the queen for trends and styles. When others hear about this, women all over the country will think, 'If the queen doesn't respect the king's commands, why should I?' And what about the rest of the world? When the news of the queen's refusal reaches them, we'll become the laughing stock of the whole world. We will have gone from the most feared and respected country to a joke in a single night all because of her!" Hayden ended dramatically, waving his hand in the air for emphasis.

"She must be disciplined," spoke a minister.

"I agree," said King Xavier. "What does the council recommend?"

"Have her removed from the palace," Malcolm, the chief minister suggested. "Have her stripped of her title as queen, divorce her, and give her position to another."

"Someone better," another minister chimed in.

The king frowned. "But I don't have time to search for another queen," he interjected. "What do you suggest about that?"

The council was silent as they thought. "Well?" the king asked impatiently."

"You could hold a competition," suggested the minister of defense. "Like the beauty pageants of old!

Have each province hold their own competition, and then the winners come to the palace, where you will be able to observe them and make a final decision."

"Yes… A contest to find the most beautiful. I like it!" The king smiled. "But she must be talented and smart as well. *She* was smart. The new queen must be smarter than *her.* Send out a decree for all beautiful unmarried women to compete. Oh, and, Minister of Communication," King Xavier said. He turned to the minister.

"Yes, Your Majesty?" the minister replied as his secretary began to quickly write some notes.

"Prepare a message about *her,* and get it to the news stations for the morning news. I want this situation taken care of now."

FOUR

Matthew answered his phone on the second ring. "Hello?" he asked.

"Matthew, it's me, Joshua. You've heard about what happened with Queen Valerie, right?"

"Of course. It's been on the news all morning."

"Well, here's what's not on the news yet. They're holding a country-wide competition where all the beautiful unmarried young women will compete for becoming the next queen."

Matthew was surprised. "You're not telling me I should sign up Hannah for the competition, are you, Joshua?"

"I'm telling you that you won't have a choice." Joshua sighed. "The king made it mandatory. They're sending troops through the city and throughout the country to gather women for each province's local competition, and then they'll bring the winning ladies to the palace for the final competition."

Matthew was silent. *Oh, LORD, what should I do?* "What are you suggesting I do then, Joshua?"

Matthew heard Joshua sigh. "Well, you could try and take her and run, but I doubt you'd get very far. I recommend keeping her inside and hidden until the competition is over. I'm part of the group that is 'rounding up' Susa's finest. I'll do what I can to keep her off the radar."

"Thank you, Joshua, for letting me know. I better go talk to Hannah," Matthew replied and ended the call.

Hannah mindlessly flipped through the television channels, not really paying attention to what might have been on. She was bored. Matthew had not allowed her to go outside for almost five days, and she felt like she was going crazy. She understood his concern, with the soldiers rounding up every young woman in the city, but at the same time she was confused. Why shouldn't she be allowed to participate in the contest? Didn't Matthew think she had what it took to be a good queen? "He's just being overprotective," Hannah said aloud and then giggled. "I've been inside by myself for so long that I'm talking to myself now! Well, no one can see me in the backyard, so it won't hurt to go out there for a little while, right?" And shutting of the TV, she went outside.

Matthew's fist slammed down on the "close" button of the garage door control. Throwing the door open to the house, he called out, "Hannah!"

"I'm in my room. I'll be right down." Hannah's voice drifted down the stairs. Matthew sighed with relief. He had seen soldiers coming down their street, and he had been afraid they might have taken her.

Hannah came down the steps. "Is everything okay? You're not usually home quite this early."

Just then the doorbell rang, followed by a loud knock on the door. "I'll get it," said Hannah as she moved to pass Matthew. He put out his hand to stop her. "No, you wait here. I'll see who it is."

Matthew moved slowly to the door. *Maybe it's just a neighbor. There's nothing to worry about,* he thought. The doorbell rang again and a loud knock, followed by, "Open in the name of the king." Matthew shut his eyes for a moment in despair. Opening his eyes, he took a deep breath and opened the door, keeping his hand firmly on the doorknob. "How might I be of service to the king?" he said to the soldier at his door.

"We were told a young woman resides here. Why hasn't she gone to the competition?" the soldier said, looking past Matthew into the house, his eyes coming to rest on Hannah.

Matthew glanced behind him and saw his cousin as well. He reached up with his other hand and grasped the doorjamb almost as if to block the doorway. "Surely you've found so many contestants already that you need no more," he said desperately.

The soldier shifted his gaze back to Matthew and shrugged. "All unmarried women must compete by order of the king. No exceptions."

Matthew realized that there was no escape. Hannah would have to go. "May I at least have a few minutes to say good-bye?"

The soldier stared at Matthew as if weighing his words. Finally he spoke. "You have ten minutes." Matthew shut the door. He turned to Hannah and held out his arms.

Hannah ran across the entryway and threw herself into his arms. "Oh, Matthew, what do I do?"

"You will go and do your best at whatever this competition has you do. But, Hannah, I need you to listen carefully. You must hide your belief in the LORD."

Hannah's voice was muffled as she spoke against his chest. "But you taught me to be proud of our faith, to not be ashamed if others make fun of us because of it."

Matthew pulled back so he could look at her. "True, my dear, but you're now involved in something bigger—much bigger than you understand right now. I wish I had thought to give you lessons in politics." He lowered his face so he could look directly into her eyes. "There are people—powerful people—who don't like those who believe in the LORD. If you were to win this competition and become queen, they would use it against you, or hold it over you and use it to control you. If you would refuse to help them, they would turn the king against you. You must keep it secret."

Hannah nodded. "I don't completely understand, but I'll do as you recommend."

"There is one more thing. Your name—it would give you away. I think you should go by your second name—Esther. Since it means 'star,' it sounds less religious and more, well, mystical. That should help protect you."

She looked up at Matthew, tears filling her eyes. "I don't want to go," she whispered.

Matthew smiled and brushed away a tear that had begun to slide down her cheek. "At least my job at the palace will allow us to see each other on occasion." Esther went upstairs to pack.

FIVE

The soldier put out his hand to help Esther out of the back of the transport. Esther put her hand in his and jumped lightly to the ground. "Go stand at the end of the line over there," the soldier said. He dropped Esther's hand and pointed to the line of young women that was snaking its way across the parking lot and into the front door of Susa University's gymnasium. Esther took her suitcase from another soldier and walked over to the line.

A sigh escaped Esther's lips as she took her place in line. The tall blonde ahead of Esther turned and looked over her shoulder. She looked Esther over and then gave a smile that didn't reach her eyes. With a flip of her silky hair, she turned back to the front of the line, stepping forward as the line began to move. Esther raised her eyebrows and moved forward five steps to where the line had stopped again. "Friendly bunch here," she murmured, amused. "Well, it is a competition, not a party." Esther set her suitcase on the ground and sat on the edge, waiting for the line to move forward.

After an hour, Esther was almost to the door. Thanking the soldier that was passing bottles of water out to the ladies in the line, she quickly twisted the cap off and drank thirstily from the bottle. Just then the line began to move, so Esther replaced the cap and grabbed her suitcase. She then entered the building, where another soldier was directing the ladies to the row of tables. Esther approached the table to which she was directed.

The man sitting at the table swiveled the computer screen to face Esther, then pointed at the touchscreen keyboard on the table in front of her. "Please enter your name as you would like it to appear in the competition," he said. Esther did so, and then he turned the screen back and slid the keyboard back in front of him. "Age?" he asked.

"I'll turn twenty-four in October," she replied.

“What’s your level of education?”

“I completed secondary education. I graduated with high honors, if that’s important.”

The man’s fingers flew across the keyboard’s surface. “What kind of talents do you possess? Any accomplishments?”

“Um, well… I sing soprano, and I can play the piano tolerably well. I learned three languages at secondary school and have stayed fluent in them. I can draw and paint pretty well.” Esther bit her lip as she thought for a moment. “Oh! I wrote an article for my school’s paper that was also published by the local news. Do you need more?”

The man did not look up from the screen. “No, that’ll be enough for now. So… ” he continued. He finished typing, then reached behind him and grabbed a computer tablet off one of the stacks there. Handing it to Esther, he said, “Find a seat in the gym and fill this out while you wait for your name to be called. “Next!” he yelled, motioning for another candidate to be sent his way. Esther picked up her suitcase and headed toward the gym.

Esther lay in the bunk to which she had been assigned, her mind swirling with the events of the day. After completing the questions on the tablet, she'd been taken to a room where she had been examined by a doctor. She'd then been led to a room where she completed a wide array of physical and mental acuity tests. Esther had felt like a lab rat when she was done. She was very glad when they had announced dinner. Afterward they had been bussed to the dormitories and told they had three hours until lights out. Esther had been so exhausted she had just flopped down on her bunk, but her mind had not slowed down enough to let her fall asleep. Lights out had come and gone and still she was awake. Esther rolled onto her side and bunched her pillow up beneath her head. *Thank you, Lord, for being with me today,* she prayed. *I don't know what your plan is with this, Lord, but I'm so grateful you'll be with me every step of the way.*

The following six days passed in much the same way. Every day their beauty and talents were tested and measured, and at the end of each day the busses returned fewer and fewer ladies to the dormitories. At the end of the week, Susa's competition was down to

Esther and twenty-four other beautiful and accomplished young ladies.

The next morning, when the ladies were finished with breakfast, the tall, thin man who had been in charge of Susa's competition rose to speak. He had always reminded Esther of a crow, with his beak-like nose and harsh, rasping voice. "Congratulations, ladies," he began, "you twenty-five are the finest, most beautiful and accomplished ladies that the District of Susa has to offer. You've the rest of today to yourselves to call or visit your family, for tomorrow you'll be taken to the palace where you will compete against the finalists from the rest of Perea's districts for the right to be crowned Queen of Perea. Good luck and represent Susa well!"

Esther got up from the cafeteria table and headed back to the dormitory to pack. She didn't want to miss the first bus out; she wanted to be able to spend as much of the day with her cousin as possible.

Wow, Lord, she prayed, *I'm a finalist. Wouldn't that be funny if the king picked me for his queen?*

SIX

King Xavier strode into Henry's office and went to the wall of television screens that had been placed there to allow Henry, the king's chief steward and the man "in charge" of the competition, to observe the contestants and advise the king on the "queenliness" of the different women.

"So what are they up to now?" asked Xavier, stopping next to Henry's chair. Henry quickly stood at the king's presence, but Xavier waved Henry back to his seat and looked at the screens.

"Well, a large group of them seem to be holding some races, sire." Henry pointed to the screen that displayed a group of women gathered together. The king watched as five ladies lined up at the edge of one of the garden pathways. A servant standing at the far end of the path gave them the signal to go, and they took off running as the onlookers cheered. A tall, graceful woman quickly took the lead and kept it all the way. At the finish line, several women came over and congratulated her. The king and Henry continued to watch as the women ran more races.

"Who is that?" Xavier asked, pointing to a woman on the screen.

Henry opened the binder that contained a dossier on each woman. "That would be Esther, from right here in Susa."

"Esther," said the king quietly. "She congratulated all the women, whether they won or not. Hmm." He turned and began to walk to the door.

"Do you want her removed from the competition?" Henry called after the king.

King Xavier paused in the doorway and rested his left hand against the doorframe. "No," he replied without turning. "Give her a gift. A necklace, perhaps."

Esther gathered up her mathematics books and supplies from her desk and slowly followed the others out of the classroom. As much as she missed her home and her cousin, Esther was pleased at the opportunities she had been given since coming to the palace. When she had first heard about the contest to find the next queen, she had thought they were looking for a "trophy queen"—just a beautiful bimbo to look good on the king's arm at political functions. And when she had arrived at the competition, it was obvious that they were looking for a woman who was beautiful. When the finalists arrived at the palace, they were told that there would be educational classes they would be able to attend to help improve their minds and turn them into knowledgeable queen candidates.

Esther had barely been able to contain her excitement. She had always dreamed of being able to go to the university. But she knew that even with financial aid, Matthew would never have been able to afford it. Yet here she was, able to take courses on all kinds of things. Esther enjoyed the botany courses in which they spent much of their time either in the palace's gardens or greenhouses. But the course she loved the most was ancient literature. She loved being able to spend hours in the palace library surrounded by books, many of which could only be found there, for many books had been destroyed in the wars before. She also liked to help the computer scribes in their task of copying books onto the digital system, which would allow the books to be sent to the digital libraries the king was having set up all over the country. "For," as the king had said when he began the project, "it is important for the people to have access to the knowledge of the past so that we learn and grow and share our knowledge. Together, we can make a better future."

Esther turned down the hall to her rooms and saw that someone was waiting at her door. As she got closer, she saw that it was Henry. "Greetings, Master Henry. May I help you with something?"

Henry smiled at Esther's greeting. Many of the women showed him little respect, for while he was in charge of the king's household, he was a servant. And even in these times, many looked down on servants.

"Lady Esther, the king wishes to give you a gift." Henry held up a wooden box and opened it, revealing several necklaces of varying sizes and jewels. "You may pick any one of these, and it is yours to keep, even if you are eliminated from the competition."

Esther reached up and gently ran a finger across the necklaces. "They are all so beautiful. I don't know what to say."

Henry shrugged but remained silent, holding the box open for her perusal. Esther picked up a necklace made of gold and turquoise beads in one hand and a string of sapphires and emeralds set in gold backings in the other. "I'm not used to such ornate jewelry. Please," she said, looking up at him, "what do you suggest, Master Henry?"

Again Henry was amazed by Esther's words. *It is a wise woman who shows such respect for her servants,* he thought. *The king would do well to consider this one for queen.*

Henry smiled and replied, "The ones you hold are much too ornate for you. Their beauty would only distract from your beauty." Reaching into the box, he pulled out a necklace with a tear-dropped-shaped emerald hanging from a single twisted golden chain. "This would add to the sparkle of your equally green eyes."

Esther let the necklaces she had been holding slip from her fingers back into the box and cupped her hands beneath the one Henry was holding. "It's perfect," she whispered. "Please thank the king for me."

"Of course," Henry replied, and with a bow, he left.

SEVEN

And so the competition continued. Every day contests were held and prizes awarded to the winners. But every day ladies were also eliminated from the competition. So it went until from the thousand women that had entered the palace, only thirty were left. The following morning Henry gathered them together in a conference room.

Henry stood before them and began to speak. "Today the final phase of the competition begins. Beginning in two months, each of you will spend a day with King Xavier. You will eat meals with him, go with him to meetings, and see what it would be like to be the queen. One of you will be chosen to be the next queen of Perea!"

And so their days changed. Gone were the days where the finalists had hours of time to spend as they wished. Now they had lessons and meetings on what it took to be a queen of Perea. They were taught how to preside over state dinners and greet foreign dignitaries. They had lessons on how to respond to questions asked them by news reporters. They spent an entire week on the laws of Perea and the policies and treaties that govern how Perea dealt and interacted with other nations in the world.

After a month, seven of the finalists had been sent home, leaving twenty-two women and Esther to continue on.

About a week later, Henry heard a knock on his office door. Opening it, he saw Esther standing before him, looking nervous and troubled. "Lady Esther, is everything all right?" he asked.

"Everything is fine," she responded. "I was just wondering if I could talk to you."

Henry stepped to the side of the doorway and motioned for Esther to enter. "Yes, of course you may talk to me. What is it that is troubling you?"

Esther sat and looked down at her hands that were clenched together in her lap and then back at

Henry, who had taken a seat as well. "Everything that we have been learning this past month has been to educate us on how to be a queen. But," she hesitated, trying to figure out the right words to explain what she was feeling and thinking, "it hasn't really prepared us for meeting with the king. What is he like? What *does* he like? Does he get angry easily, and what makes him angry? What makes him happy, and what does he like to talk about? I know you know the king well, and I'm wondering if you would be willing to help me with my questions," Esther finished quickly.

Henry sat there quietly, thinking. *Once again she has impressed me with her words and actions. No one else has asked this of me… well, ever, actually.* "I would be happy to answer your questions. Which question would you like me to answer first?"

Esther sat, staring at her reflection in the dressing table mirror but not really seeing herself. *Tomorrow is my day with the king, Lord. About half the women have already gone, and none of them were chosen. I don't know if I feel ready. What will I say? What will he say? I know that you will be with me tomorrow. Please help me to speak and act as one of your children, even though I have kept it secret from those here.*

Xavier lay in bed, staring at the ceiling. *Two weeks of women, and I haven't found the right one yet. And tomorrow I have to meet with another one.* He sighed deeply and rolled onto his side.

Esther followed Henry down the hall toward the room where King Xavier was waiting to eat breakfast with her. Her stomach felt like it was full of butterflies, and she doubted that she would really be able to eat anything.

When they reached the door, Henry knocked three swift, sharp taps. They heard the king call, "Enter." Opening the door, Henry moved to allow Esther to enter first. She took three steps into the room and stopped. There at the table before her sat the king. He wore a crisp tan suit, although his suit coat was currently draped across the back of the chair next to him. His short, curly brown hair was still slightly damp. Around his neck was an emerald-colored tie that brought out the green in his eyes.

Those green eyes came to rest on Esther, and she found herself smiling. She knew that he could be quick to anger—the whole incident with Valerie just one example—and even though she saw in those eyes the weight of concern a king should have for his country, she felt herself relax. For she saw kindness in his eyes and knew that all would be well.

Dinner was over. Esther and King Xavier had gone to the western balcony of the palace. "I've enjoyed today much more than I thought I would," Xavier said to her. "Your conversation has been most interesting."

"You've been most kind in listening as well," Esther replied, blushing.

Xavier leaned against a marble column and studied Esther, who was standing at the center of the balcony. "You are very beautiful," he said, breaking the comfortable silence that had fallen between them. Esther quickly looked down to hide her expression, but he had seen it. "What did that expression mean?" said Xavier, walking over to her and gently turning her face back up so he could study it. "Don't you believe you are beautiful?"

"I know that I have the features that people consider beautiful," Esther replied. She bit her lower lip as she considered how to say what she was thinking. "But—at least to me—it doesn't matter how beautiful a person looks if their actions are ugly."

Xavier was intrigued. "Please, explain what you mean," he urged her.

Esther took a deep breath. "Well, what good is it if a woman is very beautiful but is cruel? Here at the palace, you have hundreds of servants who work for you. Some of the women from the competition ignore them or treat them like they're nothing. But are they not people too? Are they not worthy of our care and respect?" Esther led Xavier over to the edge of the balcony and gestured downward where several gardeners could be seen caring for a flowerbed. "They are citizens of this country and deserve the same treatment we give our friends and neighbors.

"Someone is truly beautiful when they're kind to all and care about the world they live in, when they're willing to go and help others even if they'll get nothing in return." Esther rested both hands on the balcony ledge and looked toward the horizon where the sun was beginning to set. "Aren't these the qualities you're looking for in your future queen?"

Xavier smiled. "Yes, they are. I'm looking for a woman who can help guide me in doing what is best for the country. And I believe I have found her." He took her hands in his and looked into her eyes. "You, Esther, have all the qualities that we need in our queen. You are compassionate and wise, and I think I may even find myself in love with you. Will you marry me and be our queen?"

Esther looked once again into his green eyes and saw that what he said was true. "Yes," she replied simply.

EIGHT

SIX MONTHS LATER

Matthew walked down the path to the palace's walled parking lot. He was about to turn the corner into the lot when voices stopped him in his tracks. "Do you really think you can get this poison into his food tonight?" said one of the palace guards.

"I've got a shift in the palace kitchen and dining rooms tonight. It'll be easy," said a second guard. *Benedict,* Matthew realized. *They're planning to kill the king!* He turned and quietly ran back toward the palace. *I've got to warn Esther!*

There was a pause in the king and queen's conversation as Benedict set their dinners before them. The king picked up his knife and fork and began to cut his chicken into pieces. "So how are you adjusting to being queen?" Xavier asked Esther.

Esther picked up a roll and began to spread butter on it. "Pretty well, I think. It was a little overwhelming at first. I know that many adored the previous queen, and I'm sure there are some who resent that I have replaced her."

"Ah, yes," replied Xavier, "part of the consequences of being a ruler of a country. There are always people who aren't happy with the current leaders. 'You can't please all the people all the time,' or something like that was said by a leader long ago." He looked over at her. "Those rulers had to be careful of their dissenters. A bullet or a quick stab of a knife was often in their future if they weren't careful. Nowadays, current security makes sneaking a gun or knife close enough to world leaders impossible. But there is still another way to dispose of leaders if you're tricky enough."

Out of the corner of her eye, Esther saw Benedict shift nervously. "What do you mean?" she asked as she added jam to her roll.

"Poison," he responded, ignoring Benedict's visible flinch. "There are thousands of kinds and numerous ways to administer it. Did you know," he continued, stabbing a piece of chicken with his fork and holding it up, "that ancient kings and queens had food tasters to make sure that their food was safe? Benedict, how would you like to become my official food taster?" the king said, suddenly turning to him and holding his fork out. Benedict's gaze darted from the fork to the king and back, but he did not take it. "What's the matter? Is there something wrong with the chicken?" the king continued, wagging the fork up and down. Benedict opened his mouth then shut it and swallowed. His eyes dropped to the floor as the king rose from his chair. "You put poison in our dinner," King Xavier stated.

Benedict dropped to his knees before him. "Have mercy on me, oh great king!" he pleaded.

"I know you had a helper. Name your accomplice," ordered King Xavier.

"Terrence," Benedict replied.

"Guards, take this man and Terrence to prison where they will remain until a trial will determine their punishment." Xavier turned away from him as the guards grabbed Benedict by the arms and dragged him out of the room. He extended his hand to Esther.

She rose from her chair and stepped into his arms. "You've saved me, my love," he murmured into her hair.

"It was Matthew, one of the court reporters, who discovered the plot," she reminded him.

"That's right," he said, nodding. "Matthew will receive the credit in the annals."

NINE

"You called for me, sire?" Hayden said with a bow as he stopped before the king.

"Ah, yes." King Xavier smiled and motioned for him to rise. "Malcolm is retiring from his position as chief minister, and I thought I would offer you the job."

Hayden bowed deeply to the king. "I'd be honored to work with you, sire."

"Excellent!" said the king, turning back to his work. "Then you are the new chief minister. You're dismissed."

Hayden left, barely able to control his joy. This position came with great power. And Hayden liked power.

Information on Hayden's promotion was on the evening news, and by the next morning, Hayden was greeted with bows wherever he went. When he stopped at his favorite coffee shop on the way to the palace, everyone there made way and let him be served first. The owner himself waited on Hayden, and when he tried to pay, the owner refused. "We're honored that a man so favored by the king enjoys our coffee," the owner told him with a bow.

Hayden smiled in remembrance at this as he made his way into the palace. Here too he was met with bows and head nods from everyone he met. Just outside the main council room, he saw one of the court reporters. This man did not bow but looked straight at Hayden. His eyes narrowed as he stopped a few feet away from the man, and he saw just the tiniest lift of the man's chin. Hayden's anger began to rise in him, but he did not let it show.

"You there. Matthew, right?" Hayden spoke. "The king has commanded all to show me respect and honor by bowing in my presence. Why do you not bow?"

Matthew replied, "To only two do I bow: the Lord and my King. You're neither." Hayden's eyes narrowed as he glared at Matthew, willing him to bow before him. But Matthew remained straight and tall. Frustrated, Hayden turned sharply and stormed down the hall.

Hayden entered his living room and threw himself onto the couch where his wife sat, watching a movie. She paused the movie and then turned to look at Hayden. "What's bothering you, dear?" she asked, rubbing the back of his neck.

"Matthew, one of the palace reporters, refuses to bow to me and show me the proper respect because he'll only bow for 'the LORD' and the king," he said grumpily. "Those believers and their 'LORD'—who do they think they are? They think they're so much better than us with their god who does everything and takes care of them. They're a menace to our country's way of life, I tell you, and they should be gotten rid of," Hayden fumed.

His wife was quiet for a moment. "Well, you're the king's chief minister now. He listens to your advice. Maybe you could talk to him about it."

Hayden sat up, his sharp mind beginning to plan and scheme. "I could, couldn't I? But I'd have to be careful about it, come at it from the right direction. I'd have to make it not sound like genocide—that's never good for a country. Terrorists perhaps—no, believers don't like to kill. It's one of their 'commandments' or something. Sympathizers to our enemies—that might work. After all, they do believe their god is for everyone, Perean or otherwise. Yes, that might work." Hayden turned and kissed his wife on the nose. "You are truly a good wife, my love. I have to go. I must plan."

There was a knock on the king's door. "Enter," he called. Hayden opened the door and entered, bowing before the king. "You wanted to see me, Hayden," the king said. He motioned Hayden to a chair and then sat down himself. "You said you had something rather important to discuss. What is it?"

Hayden took a deep breath and began. "There's a certain group of people scattered throughout this great country whose customs and beliefs are different from those of all others. They don't obey the king's laws, and they show sympathy for all, even our enemies. I fear what might happen if we continue to tolerate these people. If there was war, these people could cause chaos inside our boarders and our enemies might succeed. Oh, great king, let a decree be issued to destroy them and save our great nation."

King Xavier's face was very grave as Hayden finished speaking. "So be it," he said.

TEN

There was a knock on Esther's door. "Enter," she called without looking up from her computer. When the door opened, she glanced over then jumped up. "Joshua!" she exclaimed, walking over to him.

He put up his hand to stop her from giving him a hug. "I don't think it's exactly appropriate for the queen to be hugging a common soldier."

Esther put her hands on her hips and sighed. "No, I guess not." She tipped her head to the side and raised an eyebrow. "What *are* you doing here?" she asked.

"Matthew needs to speak with you. He's downstairs. Will you please come?"

"Is he okay?" she asked with alarm.

Joshua held the door open for her to exit the room. "He'll explain everything. Please come."

"What is it?" Esther asked immediately upon entering the room where Matthew was waiting. She saw the distress in his face and was afraid. "Are you all right? What has happened? Please tell me!"

Matthew found he could not get his voice to work. Silently he handed Esther a copy of the decree that Hayden had written.

Esther grabbed the paper from his hand and quickly began to read. "On the thirteenth day of April…order to kill, plunder, and destroy…" Esther stopped in shock and looked at Matthew. "This says even the children are to be killed!" She thrust the paper back at Matthew. "This has to be a mistake," she said, shaking her head. "Xavier wouldn't do this."

Matthew took the paper and held it up. "But here is his signature," he said quietly, pointing to the bottom. "You need to go to him and beg for mercy and plead for your people."

Esther shook her head. "Since the attempted poisoning, no one is allowed anywhere near him without an appointment and some serious security checks, and the guards get rather snippy when I show up unannounced. Security has been on high alert lately too, with rumors of discontent, and Xavier's so busy right now dealing with the border skirmishes to our north with the country of Brangor and the floods in the south. I haven't seen him in a month."

Matthew moved to stand directly in front of Esther and took her hands in his. "Don't think that because you are the queen that you're going to escape this decree. If you do nothing, deliverance will come from somewhere else, but you and I and many others will perish. And who knows?" Matthew continued, the corners of his mouth turning up into the smallest of smiles. "Maybe the Lord brought you here for this very reason."

Esther looked up at her cousin. "Very well. Go. Gather the believers in Susa and fast and pray for me. Tomorrow I'll go to the king."

Matthew sighed with relief. "We will do so. May the Lord be with you." He kissed her on the forehead, and then he and Joshua left.

ELEVEN

The day passed too quickly for Esther. She had spent much of the day and night in prayer, yet she was still unsure of exactly what she was going to say to the king. But the time had come. She called for her maids and began her preparations to go to the king.

✾

The walk to the king's office had never felt so long to her. The hallways between her room and the office seemed to stretch even as she walked through them. Every step made her more nervous about what she was about to do. But finally she arrived.

The doorman stepped in front of the door as she approached. "Queen Esther," he said with a bow. "What can I do for you?"

Esther opened her mouth to speak, but nothing came out. She cleared her throat and tried again. "I would like to speak with the king," she said quietly, biting her lip and twisting the ring on her finger nervously.

He scanned the list of names in his hand. "I'm sorry," he replied. "You're not on the list. You know the rules."

Suddenly, in the blink of an eye, no longer was a nervous young woman standing before the doorman but a calm, commanding queen. "You will let me pass," she said. He did not attempt to stop her as she moved past him and opened the door; instead, he bowed. "Good luck, my queen," he whispered as she entered the king's office.

The office was full of security officers, secretaries, councilmen, a news crew, and of course, King Xavier. He looked up with annoyance from the papers he had been studying. His expression turned to surprise as he watched Esther enter.

She took a step and then another. Then Esther stumbled and fell to her knees, bracing her hands against the floor to keep from falling completely flat. She heard the sound of weapons being drawn from their hiding places and footsteps as the king's bodyguards moved between her and the king, preparing to protect him from any possible threat. Esther did not move from her position but continued to stare at the floor as the others in the room quieted and turned to the king to see his response.

"Stand down!" ordered the king as he moved from behind his desk. The guards stepped aside and holstered their weapons. Xavier came and stood in front of Esther. There he squatted down before her and reached out with a hand to lift her chin so he could look into her eyes. He spoke softly to her. "What is it, my dear? Why are you here? What do you want? Even if it costs half the kingdom, I'll give it to you."

Esther gazed into the eyes of her husband and King. She knew she could not say what was needed in front of all those people. "If it pleases the king," she answered, "will you and Hayden come to a dinner I've prepared?"

King Xavier looked over his shoulder where one of his secretaries stood. "Send for Hayden," he said. Turning back to Esther, he pulled her to her feet and replied, "We'll be there in an hour."

The king and Hayden ate heartily at Esther's dinner. She had asked the kitchen staff to make some of the favorite dishes of both men.

After dessert had been served, the king turned to Esther. "I have a suspicion that this meal was not your real reason for coming to see me in my office earlier today." Xavier smiled as Esther bit her lip and ducked her head. "Ah, yes, I was correct." He reached across the table to where her hand rested on the table's surface and placed his hand over hers. "Now what is it that you need, dearest? Whatever it is, you may have it. What is your request? Even if it costs half the kingdom, it'll be yours."

Esther glanced at Hayden and back to the king. She opened her mouth to speak and then closed it again and began to chew on her lower lip. *Help me, LORD! What do I say? I'm not ready yet. I need more time. That's it! A little more time.*

Esther placed her other hand over the king's hand already covering hers. "If it's all right and pleases you, will you and Hayden come tomorrow to another dinner I will prepare for you? Then I'll answer your question."

The king looked at Hayden. "I'd be honored," replied Hayden.

"Tomorrow it is, then," said the king.

TWELVE

Hayden flung open the door to his house with enough force that it bounced off the wall and swung shut behind him.

"What's the matter, darling?" his wife asked, looking up from the book she had been reading on her tablet computer.

"Matthew! He still refuses to show me the proper respect even after I'm the only person besides the king that Queen Esther invited to a dinner party she gave."

His wife waved a hand through the air. "Build a gallows and have him hanged," she suggested.

Hayden looked at her with derision. "No one hangs people nowadays," he scoffed.

She shrugged and returned to her reading. "Sometimes the old ways are the best ways," she replied. Hayden continued to look at her thoughtfully for a minute then slowly walked to the window, his mind swirling with thoughts.

It was late, and Xavier was unable to sleep. He was lying on a bed in the spare room nearest his office, where he had slept for the last two weeks so he would not wake Esther after working so late. He tried counting the stars he could see through the window of the room, but it didn't work.

Finally he threw himself out of bed and called for a servant to bring a copy of Perea's annals. Xavier had always felt that the annals were always written in the most dry and boring wording imaginable. Perhaps the quiet droning voice of the man reading them aloud would lull him to sleep.

The servant returned, sat down, and began to read. Xavier lay back on the bed and listened with his eyes closed. Soon the servant reached the record of how Matthew had exposed the plot to assassinate the king by poisoning. After the servant had read the punishment given to the would-be assassins, Xavier spoke. "What honor and reward was Matthew given for his service?"

The servant scanned the rest of the page. "It would appear that nothing has been done for him, sire," he answered.

The king frowned, opened his eyes, and sat up. "Nothing?" The servant shook his head. "Well, that won't do."

Just then, there was a knock on the door. Xavier motioned to one of the two bodyguards standing by the door to see who it was and rose from the bed. "Hayden wishes to speak with you," the bodyguard told the king.

"Let him come in," Xavier replied.

Hayden entered the room and bowed. Xavier spoke first, "Hayden, good! I have a question and could use your help in answering it. What should be done for someone the king wants to honor?"

Hayden thought to himself, *After all that I've done and am going to do for Perea, who else could the king mean but me?* Hayden smiled and replied, "Oh, gracious king, have one of your council members announce to the world what the man has done for the king on the morning news. Reward him with fine clothes and a new car, which should be presented to him on the morning news as well. That way all will know how it is for those who serve the king."

The king replied, "I agree. It's a fitting reward for Matthew."

The smile fell from Hayden's face but was replaced with another so quickly it went unnoticed by the king. "Matthew, sire?" he managed to say.

"Yes. Matthew. He was the one who uncovered the assassination plot," Xavier said, motioning for the door to be opened so Hayden could exit. "I want you to go and do just as you've suggested for Matthew."

Hayden bowed and silently left the room, stunned at the turn of events.

THIRTEEN

Hayden left the news studio and sped toward home. As he impatiently waited for a red light to turn green, he found the events of the morning haunting his thoughts. He felt the heat of shame creep into his face, so he stomped on the accelerator as soon as the light turned.

He whipped his car into his driveway and turned off the engine. His wife was standing just inside the front door waiting for him. Her arms were folded across her chest, and her eyes were filled with worry. "She saw it," he muttered, rubbing his eyes.

He was about to open the car door when his cell phone beeped, causing him to jump. He checked his message and groaned. He needed to get ready right away or he would be late for the queen's dinner party. "Can this day get any worse?" he asked himself as he got out of the car.

The king and Hayden again joined Esther for her second banquet. The king ate heartily while Hayden was rather subdued and only picked at his bread. "What's troubling you today, Hayden?" Xavier asked.

Hayden gave the king a smile. "Nothing at all, my king. I'm just a little tired. I had a long night last night."

Xavier waved at the food-laden table before them. "Well, have something to eat. I'm sure it will help perk you up. What do you recommend, my dear?" he finished, turning to Esther.

Esther smiled warmly at the king and motioned for a cup of coffee to be brought to Hayden.

Hayden took a drink from the cup and began to eat. The king, now satisfied with Hayden, turned back to Esther. "Now, my dear Queen Esther, what is your petition? Whatever it is, I'll give it to you. What is it you request? Even if it were to cost me half the kingdom, it's yours."

Esther took a deep breath and replied. "Oh great king, I ask that you grant me my life. That's my petition. And spare the lives of the people like me. That's my request. For we've been given a death sentence because of our faith in the LORD. If we'd merely been exiled from Perea or even sold as slaves, I would've kept quiet. But we're to be annihilated—men, women, and children."

As Esther spoke, King Xavier's face darkened with anger while Hayden's had become pale with fear. King Xavier rose slowly from his chair. "Who has done this?" he asked through clenched teeth. "Who has dared to do such a thing?"

Esther stretched out her arm and pointed at Hayden, who sat frozen in his chair with a fork raised to his mouth. "It is Hayden who has ordered our destruction," she said calmly.

Silently the king turned and left the room, his anger almost visible in his wake. For a moment, the room was silent. The fork that had been in Hayden's hand suddenly slipped from his grasp, hit the edge of the table, and clattered to the floor, startling both Esther and himself.

Hayden knew that he was in deep trouble. Rising from his chair, he began to move toward Esther. She also stood and began to back away from him, for she saw in his eyes the crazed look of terror mixed with desperation, and she was afraid of him.

"Queen Esther, had I known… surely you don't… Please… " Hayden started and stopped, unable to complete a thought or sentence in his terror.

Esther opened her mouth to call for a guard, when suddenly Hayden lunged forward, wrapping his arms around Esther's legs just below her knees. "Mercy!" he shrieked.

A small cry of surprise escaped Esther's lips as she lost her balance and began to fall. Just as Esther hit the floor, the doors flew open. King Xavier and two palace guards entered the room. Seeing Esther on the floor with Hayden pinning her down, the king's anger burned within him. "Does his evil know no bounds? Will he even attack the queen while I'm in the palace?"

The guards immediately hauled Hayden up off the floor and the queen and bound his hands behind his back. Then one of the guards, who had been on duty the night before, spoke up. "It may interest you to know, Your Majesty, that when Hayden came to speak with you last night, he meant to ask for your permission to hang Matthew, the man who uncovered the assassination plot."

King Xavier spoke. "His punishment will be of his own design. Hang him." The guards then dragged Hayden from the room.

In two steps, Xavier was at Esther's side. "Are you all right, my love?" he asked, gently helping her to her feet and then pulling her close.

"I am now," she responded, wrapping her own arms around him. "I am now."

FOURTEEN

Matthew entered the room where Esther and the king were waiting for him. When Esther saw him, she jumped up from the couch where she had been sitting with the king and ran to Matthew. She grabbed his hand and pulled him over to where the king now stood.

"Xavier, this is my cousin Matthew. He raised me after my parents were killed. He's like a second father to me."

Matthew bowed to the king, but Xavier reached out and grasped Matthew's hand. "It's a pleasure to meet you. You were also the man who exposed the assassination plot. It seems I owe you much."

Matthew shook the king's hand. "You're welcome."

King Xavier then continued. "You have shown yourself to be a wise and caring person. I'd like for you to take the position of chief minister that has become vacant due to Hayden's treachery."

Matthew smiled and once again shook the king's hand. "It would be an honor to be able to serve my country in such a way. Thank you! I accept."

Just then Esther began to cry. Xavier cradled her face in his hands. "Why are you crying, dearest? What's troubling you?"

Esther replied, "Even though Hayden's dead, his edict still lives on. All who believe in the LORD are still in danger. I beg of you to make another edict that would overrule the order given by Hayden. Because I couldn't bear to see the destruction of my family and all those who believe as we do."

King Xavier turned to Matthew. "Go. Write a decree in my name. Word it as you see fit. Bring it to me, and I'll sign it, that way all will know it comes from me and is to be obeyed."

Matthew bowed to the king. "Thank you, King Xavier. I'll go and do so immediately."

The day of the edict came. Xavier and Esther sat together on a stone bench in the palace gardens. Soon Matthew joined them, and Esther looked up at her cousin. "What's the latest news? I had rather hoped that knowing the people would retaliate would keep us from being attacked. Do you think many will die?"

Matthew looked at Esther. "Numbers are coming in. There have been casualties on both sides. There are always people who will be tempted by the chance of getting the wealth of others, even if they have to fight for it. The LORD knew that his people would be in danger. He put you here so he could save us, and he has."

> King Xerxes imposed tribute throughout the empire, to its distant shores, and all his acts of power and might, together with a full account of the greatness of Mordecai to which the king had raised him, are they not written in the book of the annals of the kings of Media and Persia?
>
> Esther 10:1–2 (NIV)